Mouse & Mole

and the All-Weather Train Ride

Scientific American Books for Young Readers is an imprint of
W. H. Freeman and Company, 41 Madison Avenue, New York, NY 10010.

Library of Congress Cataloging-in-Publication Data

Cushman, Doug.

Mouse and Mole and the all-weather train ride / by Doug Cushman.

p. cm.

Summary: Mole promises Mouse a surprise as the two friends enjoy a train
ride across the country and encounter all kinds of weather along the way.

ISBN 0-7167-6600-0 (hardcover)

[1. Mice—Fiction. 2. Moles (Animals)—Fiction. 3. Weather—Fiction.
4. Railroads—Trains—Fiction.] I. Title.

PZ7.C959Mj 1995

[E]—dc20   95-30863

                                                                  CIP

10 9 8 7 6 5 4 3 2 1   AC

For Rick and Patty, who like train rides

Mouse & Mole

and the All-Weather Train Ride

by Doug Cushman

Scientific
American
BOOKS FOR YOUNG READERS

W. H. FREEMAN AND COMPANY/ NEW YORK

Early one rainy morning Mouse carried his suitcase to Mole's house.

"I'm ready for our train trip," said Mouse. "But why won't you tell me what my surprise is?"

"Because then it wouldn't be a surprise," said Mole. "Now let's hurry to the train station."

WHAT IS WEATHER?

The day-to-day changes in these things make up the weather.

Sun

Water

Clouds

Wind

Air pressure (weight)

By the time the two friends arrived at the station, they were soaked. As they climbed onto the train, the conductor called out, "All aboard!" The train began to move.

"Here we go," said Mole.

THE WATER CYCLE

We never run out of water. It is used over and over.

Evaporation

Water rises into air as gas (vapor).

Condensation

Water vapor turns into tiny droplets, forming clouds.

Precipitation

Water drops fall back to Earth.

Mouse and Mole found their seats inside their very own compartment and pulled off their wet rain gear.

"Will we be there soon?" asked Mouse.

"No," said Mole. "It's a long ride."

"What can we do while we're riding?" asked Mouse.

KINDS OF PRECIPITATION

RAIN
(water drops)

SLEET
(partly frozen raindrops)

HAIL
(ice-layered raindrops)

SNOW
(ice crystals formed on water droplets)

"We can eat, read, play games, or just look out the window," said Mole.

"What's out the window?" asked Mouse.

"Go take a look," said Mole.

THUNDER AND LIGHTNING

Lightning is electricity in the air.

Water droplets move around in a cloud.

They move faster and faster. As they rush past each other...

an electric spark is made.

It jumps from the cloud!

Suddenly lightning flashed. Thunder boomed.

"I hate thunder and lightning," said Mouse. "Will they follow us on our trip?"

"I don't believe so," said Mole. "In the meantime, try to think of the storm as a giant fireworks show."

When lightning flashes... it heats the air. The air expands very quickly and BOOM! You hear thunder!

As the train sped along the track, the thunder and lightning stopped. So did the rain.

"I'm hungry," said Mouse.

CLOUDS

Clouds are made of tiny drops of water.

Water evaporates from the ground.

In the cool air, the vapor becomes tiny droplets of water.

They stick together with dust in the air and form clouds.

"We can get something to eat in the dining car,"
said Mole.

As they ate, the sun came out from behind a cloud.

"Look!" cried Mouse. "A rainbow!"

HOW TO SEE A RAINBOW

The sun must
be behind you,
and low in the sky.

Tiny water drops must
be in front of you.

The sunlight
is bent and you
see different
colors.

The train zoomed along the tracks. Mouse saw some boats on the lake, their sails filled with the wind.

WIND

Wind starts when warm air rises.

Cool air flows in to fill the space that's left.

This moving air is the wind!

Earth spinning in space helps move the air.

MEASURING THE WIND

A cup anemometer measures wind speed.

A weathervane (wind vane) shows wind direction.

A wind sock shows wind speed and direction.

Soon the train stopped at a station.
"Are we there yet?" asked Mouse.
"No," said Mole. "But we have time to do some
sightseeing before the train leaves. Let's go."

The NEWS

TORNADO HITS MIDWEST

The TIMES

HURRICANE OVER OCEAN

TORNADO	Warm air rises quickly inside a thundercloud.	The air meets high winds, and begins to spin...	making a tornado funnel that reaches to Earth.
A tornado is a strong, dangerous windstorm.			

HURRICANE

A hurricane is a powerful storm that starts over water.

Warm, moist air rises above the water.

Strong winds start the air whirling.

The storm spins faster.

It may stay at sea or come ashore.

They climbed up to the top of a hill and looked down over a foggy valley.

"The valley looks like it's wearing a blanket," said Mouse. "Can we stay here for a while?"

"No," said Mole. "It will be dark soon. Let's get back to the train."

FOG

Fog is a cloud near the ground.

When air near the ground cools down...

the water vapor becomes tiny drops of water, forming fog.

 When the sun warms the fog, it turns back into vapor.

When they returned to the train, Mouse and Mole
ate dinner as they watched the moon rise over the
mountains.

Mouse yawned. "I'm sleepy," he said.

"Let's pull out our beds and go to sleep," said Mole.

And they did.

WEATHER ON THE MOON

The moon has no air or water.
Nothing can live
or grow there.

Days are very hot.
Nights are very cold.

There is no wind,
so the weather
never changes.

The next morning when Mouse woke up, he noticed the train wasn't moving. He peered out the window.

"Look!" he cried. "It's snowing!"

"We're in the mountains now," said Mole. "We're so high up that the air is much colder."

MOUNTAIN WEATHER

The higher up you go, the colder it gets.

The air is thinner.

The winds are stronger.

Very high mountains are always snow-covered.

While the train workers shoveled snow off the track, Mouse and Mole went outside to play in the snow.

"It sure is cold," said Mouse.

Suddenly the conductor cried, "All aboard!"

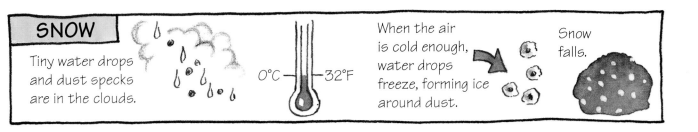

SNOW

Tiny water drops and dust specks are in the clouds.

0°C — 32°F

When the air is cold enough, water drops freeze, forming ice around dust.

Snow falls.

DESERTS

Deserts
get very
little rain...

so they are very dry.

Some deserts
are hot.

Some are cold.

Sonoran Desert

South Pole

The train rolled along. It chugged out of the mountains and down into the hot, dry desert. There wasn't a cloud in the sky. Mouse and Mole looked at the tall cactuses and felt the hot sun through the window.

CACTUS

To stay alive, a cactus must store water.

Roots are close to the surface to collect the water.

Inside, the pulpy stem holds water.

Thick walls slow evaporation.

Thorns protect the cactus from thirsty animals.

DESERT SURVIVAL

Desert animals work hard to survive in hot, dry weather.

Some get water from seeds.

Kangaroo rat

Some go underground to hide from the hot sun.

Tarantula

Most feed at night, when it is cooler.

Coyote

Soon the train pulled into a tiny station.

"It sure is hot," said Mouse. "Maybe we can cool off in that lake over there."

Mole smiled. "Look again," he said. "It's not a real lake. It's a mirage."

MIRAGE

Is there really water?

Hot, thin air near the ground bends light from the sky.

Light from sky

Bent light

Warm air

What looks like water is really a reflection of the sky.

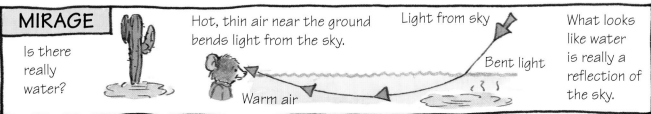

The next morning the train pulled into a station in a city.

"Are we there yet?" asked Mouse.

"Yes," said Mole.

They collected their bags and walked out onto a busy street.

"Is this where my surprise is?" asked Mouse.

"You'll see," said Mole.

Le Chic

GREENHOUSE

A greenhouse stays warm by trapping heat.

Sunlight goes through the glass.

Plants take in the sunlight and give off heat.

The heat is trapped by the glass.

GREENHOUSE EFFECT

Earth acts as a greenhouse.  The air is like the glass. Land and water take in the sunlight and give off heat.  The air traps the heat.

Mouse followed Mole to a tall building. A voice called out, "Mole! You've finally arrived!"

"Mouse, this is my uncle Arvid," said Mole. "He is the weather mole here at the TV station."

"What a great surprise!" said Mouse. "Nice to meet you."

"Would you like to take a tour of the station?" asked Uncle Arvid.

"Oh, yes!" cried Mouse.

And they did.

 **SMOG**

Smog is dirty fog.

 Smoke mixes with water drops in fog.

The dirt and smoke make the fog heavy...

 and keep it close to the ground.

GLOBAL WARMING

Smog and other kinds of air pollution add to Earth's greenhouse effect.

Dirt in the air acts like a roof.

Heat can't escape.

Uncle Arvid showed Mouse and Mole all the equipment
he used as the weather mole.

STUDYING THE WEATHER

Weather scientists
have many ways to
learn about weather.

IN
THE
AIR

 A weather
satellite takes
a picture of Earth
from space.

 A weather
balloon carries
instruments to
measure winds
in upper air.

After the tour Uncle Arvid said, "Now I have a surprise for both of you. Let me drive you there."

ON THE GROUND  A thermometer measures air temperature. A barometer measures air pressure. A hygrometer measures the amount of water vapor in the air. A rain gauge measures rainfall.

They pulled up to an airport, and Uncle Arvid led them to a small plane.

"Is this the surprise?" asked Mouse.

"Yes," said Uncle Arvid. "I am going to fly you back home."

"From the sky, we'll be able to see everywhere we've been," said Mole.

"Climb aboard!" said Uncle Arvid. "Get ready for takeoff!"

JET STREAMS

A jet stream is a narrow, fast wind in the upper air.

Jet streams move in paths over Earth.

They help speed airplanes on their way.

Jet streams move weather across Earth.

Tomorrow the weather we have now will move on.

And we will get the weather someone else has today!

And they did.